Shoo Rayner

ROMAN
BRIT

STINKIUS MAXIMUS

ORCHARD BOOKS
338 Euston Road, London NW1 3BH
Orchard Books Australia
Level 17/207 Kent Street, Sydney, NSW 2000

First published in 2015 by Orchard Books
ISBN 978 1 40833 446 1

A CIP catalogue record for this book is available
from the British Library.

1 3 5 7 9 10 8 6 4 2

Printed in Great Britain

Orchard Books is an imprint of Hachette Children's Group
and published by The Watts Publishing Group Limited, an Hachette UK company.

www.hachette.co.uk

Shoo Rayner

ROMAN
BRIT

STINKIUS MAXIMUS

ORCHARD

FORT FINIS TERRAE is a sleepy backwater in the great Roman Empire. A young shepherd boy named Brit lives there with his sheep and faithful dog Festus.

It's a quiet life for Brit and his animals in the fort. But every so often, something happens to make it a day to remember!

GERMANIA

A

ARABIA

CHAPTER ONE

"What do you mean I can't go to the toilet?!"

Drusilla's piercing voice echoed through the cold and empty bath house.

The icicles on the ceiling tinkled. One broke off, fell silently through the air and shattered on the frozen bath water below. Festus barked and chased the broken bits across the ice.

"We can't leave the fort," Brit explained.

"There's too much snow!"

It was the worst winter anyone could remember. Fort Finis Terrae was surrounded by deep, thick drifts of snow. Worst of all, they had run out of firewood, and no one could get in or out of the gates to get any more.

Brit had left the barn where he lived and moved his sheep into the centre of the fort, where they would be safe until the snow thawed.

The courtyard of the fort looked more like a farmyard than the nerve centre of a highly disciplined fighting force. Brit spent most of the time clearing up sheep poo and throwing it over the castle walls into the icy sea below.

"But I need to gooooooo!" Drusilla wailed.

The icy wind whistled through the frozen corridors of Fort Finis Terrae. The storm outside blew flurries of snow through the windows of the bath house.

Drusilla was not happy. She sniffed loudly and then wrinkled her cold, red nose. "What's that awful smell?"

"Blocked drains," Brit sighed. "And cabbages. It's been such a hard winter, there are only cabbages left to eat. Cabbage is so stinky – and now the toilets have frozen solid!"

Drusilla stamped on the tail of a dolphin on the mosaic-covered floor. "So there are no toilets? Oh, I hate this place! If we were in Rome, it would be like summer now. I need to go! I'm bursting!"

"The only way in or out of the fort is through the tunnel that leads to the beach below the fortress walls," Brit explained. "Some people are using the sand dunes on the beach as toilets. But you can't go out there now – not while this storm is raging."

"I have to!" Drusilla stamped again, even though her legs were crossed. "I just can't wait! I have to go right now!" she insisted.

Drusilla's dad was the Fort Commander, so Drusilla thought she was in charge of everything.

Brit sighed. "Then I'd better come with you in case you get lost or have an accident."

Brit wasn't really Drusilla's friend, and he wasn't her servant either, but he didn't want her getting lost in the middle of the storm. Drusilla was Drusilla. She was a part of his life – whether he liked it or not.

CHAPTER TWO

As Brit and Drusilla made their way to the
beach, the sound of giant waves, crashing
on the seashore, howled through the tunnel.
When the weather was better, ships would
arrive here, and their goods would be
transported up the tunnel into the fort.

The wind whistled and howled around
them. Their flaming torches flickered. Festus's
ears streamed behind him.

Icy cold water lapped around their feet. "The tide is coming in!" Brit shouted to make himself heard over the wind. "The mouth of this tunnel is a cave, which floods during storms and high tides. You've got just enough time to do your business and get back before the cave floods and blocks off the tunnel."

The howling wind scoured their faces
with sand as they stumbled across the
beach to where the dunes began.

"I'll wait here!" Brit yelled in Drusilla's
ear. "Be quick, and come straight back!"

Drusilla disappeared behind a snow-
covered sand dune. Brit climbed the rocks
and looked the other way.

The sea was a luminous shade of green-grey against the dark blues and purples of the stormy skies. Brit watched the water writhing and twisting wildly.

Festus appeared on top of a dune, barking madly, staring out to sea.

Brit blinked the stinging salt out of his eyes. There was something out there, far out at sea. What was it? A bird? A seal? A piece of driftwood? A ship…? A ship!

"By Neptune!" Brit yelled at the storm. "They'll be smashed against the rocks! We need help!" He turned towards the sand dunes. "Droooo-s-i-i-illa-a-a-a-a-ah!"

A faint cry answered him. "I haven't finished yet!"

Festus bounded up to him, barking with alarm.

Brit held Festus's shaggy fur and looked deep into his eyes.

"I can't leave her," he said solemnly to his faithful dog. "You'll have to get help for us, while I stay here."

Brit tied seaweed to his collar and pointed at the gaping cave mouth. "Quick, boy! Go!"

With the wind behind him, Festus ran like a demon. The tide was rising quickly. Each breaking wave slung great carpets of foaming water higher and higher up the beach – they needed to head back as soon as possible.

Brit paced up and down the beach. Should he do something more? Would the soldiers follow Festus? How much longer would it be before they arrived? The boat was getting closer and closer to the rocky shore! He felt helpless.

It seemed like hours had gone by before Festus raced back across the beach towards Brit. A troop of soldiers ran after him, carrying ropes and grappling hooks.

"Well done, boy!" Brit gave Festus a huge, wet hug.

The beach was filled with soldiers,
helplessly watching as the raging sea
threw the ship from side to side. The cries
of the terrified sailors could be heard
above the howl of the wind and the
crashing of the waves.

Another sound sent shivers through them. An eerie, ghostly trumpeting, fading in and out with the rise and swell of the waves.

"What in the name of Jove is that?" Bumptius Matius, the Chief Engineer, bellowed.

The soldiers began arguing among themselves.

"Sea monsters!" one of them whimpered.

"It's Neptune, come to take us to a watery grave!" said another, cowering and falling to his knees. "We're all doomed!"

Brit lived with animals. He recognised that sound – it was the sound of an animal in fear of its life. But what sort of creature made a sound that loud?

Above the rising pandemonium, Drusilla's voice came ringing loud and clear.

"I've finished!"

CHAPTER THREE

Drusilla ran up to Brit and cowered behind him. They watched as the ship lurched up and down with the swell of the waves. A serpent-like silhouette flailed above the ship's deck.

"Is that a sea snake?" Drusilla whimpered.

"I don't know what it is," said Brit, clearing snowflakes from his eyes. "But I think we're going to find out quite soon. They're going to crash onto the shore!"

The sailor's shouts were clearer now. Brit felt he could almost reach out and touch them. "We're on a mission for the Emperor!" the captain called.

Bumptius tied a lead weight to a thin piece of cord, and tied the other end to a stronger, thicker rope.

He swung the weight round and round his head, building speed all the time. "For the Emperor!" he yelled.

Letting go, he flung the weight high into the stormy skies, through the air and onto the ship.

As the cord slapped down across the deck, the sailors grabbed hold of it. They pulled and pulled until the strong rope began snaking its way towards them through the waves.

"Make the rope tight!" Bumptius called.
The sailors tied the rope and the
soldiers heaved and hauled the ship away
from the sharp, jagged rocks and towards
the beach.

The ship came closer. Bumptius flung
ropes with hooks across the ship's bows.
Brit and Drusilla joined the soldiers,
heaving on the ropes, guiding the ship to
the sandy shore.

The wind screamed. The vessel creaked
and groaned. An almighty wave lifted the
ship high into the air, where it seemed to
hang for several long, impossible seconds.

"Look out!"
Bumptius yelled.
"Hold the ropes
tight. Don't let it
get washed back
out to sea."

"It's going to
crash onto the
beach!" Brit cried.

The giant wave melted away. The ship
smashed onto the foaming sand. Anything
that wasn't tied down on the deck was
scattered across the beach. The injured
sailors wailed and cried as they scrambled
to safety.

"Tie the ropes to the rocks," Bumptius
ordered. Make sure the ship can't float
away again."

Drusilla stood open-mouthed, pointing towards the deck of the ship. Brit followed her gaze.

He saw what Drusilla was pointing at and felt his blood turn to ice. A huge, grey shape was looming out of the wreckage. It looked like a giant snake, thrashing above the head of an enormous monster.

Brit stood rooted to the spot, open-mouthed in awe. All his life he had listened to sailors' tales of terrible monsters that roamed the seas, but none of those stories had prepared him for the sight of this beast – the beast currently charging towards him and Drusilla!

Festus ran at his master, pushing him out of the way. As he tumbled, Brit

grabbed Drusilla, pulling her into a bank of snow. The monster charged past them, crashing into the ground where they had been standing only moments before.

The ship's captain staggered along the beach. Blood poured from his head. "That's…an elephant," he croaked. "She… belongs…to the Emperor. Don't…let her… escape." The poor man's eyes rolled back in his head as he collapsed into the arms of two strong soldiers.

The elephant was easy to track in the snow. Warily, Brit and Festus followed the pathway carved out by those enormous feet.

No one tried to stop him. Everyone knew that Brit had a way with animals.

Brit found the elephant shivering behind a large sand dune, trying to find some shelter from the vicious wind. "There she is, Festus," he whispered. "Stay here, boy."

Brit hummed the tune he sang to his sheep to keep them calm, as he edged ever closer to the enormous beast. The elephant's colossal head turned towards him. A huge, brown eye watched him, deciding if he was friend or foe.

Brit spoke gently. "Hello." He knew how to talk to animals. It wasn't the words, or the language, but a tone of voice – spoken with an honest, open heart.

Still humming, he carefully placed his hand on the elephant's shoulder. The grey, craggy skin quivered beneath his touch.

Brit always had bits of old carrot in his pocket as treats for animals. He took one out and held it in the air. The snake on the elephant's head came towards the carrot and sniffed it. Then it picked the carrot up and put it in the elephant's mouth.

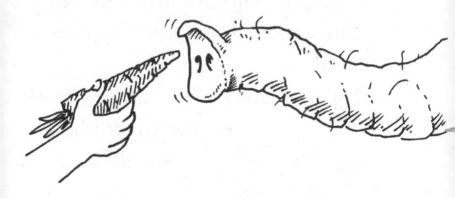

Brit realised that it wasn't a snake, but a very long nose!

He laughed as the nose began sniffing his hair and tickling his ears. But his laughter soon turned into a worried frown.

"How am I going to get you out of here before we all freeze to death?" he murmured to his new friend. "You won't squeeze into the tunnel. I'll have to guide you up the through the sand dunes and round to the Fortress gates... But how?"

The elephant's nose found Brit's pocket, reached inside and snaffled the other pieces of carrot.

"Hey!" Brit laughed. "That tickles!" Before

 he'd finished the words, the great long nose had curled itself around him, picked him off the floor and sat him high on the beast's shoulders.

Drusilla followed Brit's footsteps and approached the elephant nervously. "Is it s-s-safe up there?"

"I think so," said Brit warily.

"The t-t-tide has flooded the c-c-cave." Drusilla looked small and frightened. Her teeth were chattering. "E-e-everyone's t-t-trapped on the beach. S-s-some of the sailors are b-b-badly wounded."

The elephant picked Drusilla up too and

placed her on its back behind Brit. "Erk!" she squeaked.

"I hope elephants are like donkeys," said Brit. "I know how to make *them* move!" He gently pushed his heels into the elephant's sides and pointed forwards.

"Heya," he said in a quiet, firm voice.

The elephant moved forward slowly and

steadily. It ploughed through the snow as if there had only been a light smattering, not the deep drifts that had kept them trapped inside the fort for weeks.

Brit turned round and called to Festus. "Go and get the others, boy! Tell them to follow us."

At the entrance to Fort Finis Terrae, the elephant lowered its head and pushed the giant gates wide open.

It plodded through the courtyard, frightening the sheep and scattering chickens in all directions.

The elephant's long, snaky nose sniffed and searched until it found what it was looking for – the store of cabbages inside the kitchen door.

Brit and Drusilla laughed, and so did the soldiers inside the kitchen.

"He can have all the cabbages he wants!" one cried happily. "Look at all this delicious food we've got!"

"The ship was on its way to Londinium," another explained, "for the Emperor's birthday. So it was full of exotic birthday treats – which the captain says we can all share!"

Brit and Drusilla gazed around at the sumptuous food. Could it really be true? No more stinky cabbages for dinner?

A tired but happy-looking sailor came up to them. "It was the least we could do," he smiled. "After all, you saved us – and our elephant, Montana – from a watery grave!"

Brit and Drusilla beamed at the sailor. The kitchen filled up with more and more soldiers, holding out their bowls and cheering.

"No more cabbages!" they cried, tucking into wine, olives, dried meat and fruits.

Brit picked up a plate and joined in. He looked at Montana, who was happily munching the cabbages.

"Well," he chuckled, "you mean, no more cabbages for some of us!"

CHAPTER FOUR

The next day, it was crisp, bright and sunny. Brit and Drusilla sat high on Montana's shoulders in the courtyard of Fort Finis Terrae. The storm was just a memory, but the fort was still cold, and the drains still blocked. But Brit had had an idea…

"Open the gate!" he ordered, digging his heels into Montana's sides. "Follow us to the forest. We'll soon have firewood to warm ourselves up with!"

A gang of soldiers and citizens followed Montana, as she drove a path through the deep snowdrifts. Armed with saws and axes, they trod carefully around the massive piles of poo that she left behind her.

"Phwoar!" Drusilla wrinkled her nose. "I don't know which smells worse, cabbage stink or elephant poo!"

"Come on, Montana," Brit ordered, when they had reached the forest. "Push these trees down so they can be chopped up for firewood.

Soon enough, they were back at the fort, carrying enormous piles of wood.

Bumptius was waiting for him at the furnace of the hypercaust, a network of spaces under the floors that would be filled with hot air to heat the rooms and baths above.

"Well done, Brit!" he said, once the fires were lit and the flames were roaring.

"Thanks to you, the fort is starting to warm up again."

With a proud feeling of a job well done, Brit scooped warm water out of the public bath and filled up the sheep trough. His poor sheep hadn't had a proper drink for weeks.

Festus wanted a drink too, but when Montana saw the steam rising from the trough, she plopped her nose in and sucked up all the water!

"That's a clever trick!" Brit laughed, filling up the trough again.

"Yes," said Bumptius, but he wasn't smiling. Brit looked up at him in concern.

"The heating is back on, but we've got a big problem with the lavatorium," Bumptius explained. "The toilet drains are still blocked with frozen poo. We need someone small to climb down there and clean them out."

Brit's eyes widened in horror as Bumptius handed him a spade. "Someone small," he repeated, "like you."

CHAPTER FIVE

Brit recoiled at the thought of climbing down and cleaning out the ghastly pit of doom in the lavatorium. If only he could find another way of loosening the blockage! He watched Montana drinking and sighed. Then a brilliant idea popped into his mind.

Brit began to collect warm water from the baths. "I don't think we need a spade to clear out the drain," he said thoughtfully, as he filled up the trough. Brit dipped the end of Montana's nose in the warm water. "Drink up," he whispered in her giant ears. "Take a really big trunkful."

Bumptius led the way to the lavatorium and pointed under the toilet seats. "The

blockage is right down there," he said, "in that dark, stinky hole."

Brit turned to Montana and took her trunk in his hands. "If I hold your nose like this," he said to her, "and just tickle the end of your nose like this…"

The elephant began to wriggle and squirm and shake with the tickling. She screwed up her eyes as spasms of laughter rippled up and down her huge grey hide. Finally, with one enormous whoosh, a huge blast of warm, steaming water exploded from her nostrils and shot down the stinky drain.

Everyone held their breath and waited in silence. Then, a hideous sucking noise reverberated from the grim entrance of the drainage hole. A loud gurgle echoed round the lavatorium.

Festus stared at the drain and growled.

"That sounds like ten soldiers' stomachs rumbling after three weeks of eating only cabbage!" Brit laughed.

Then, with a loud and final POP!, the sludge began to move and the drains were running freely again.

Half the inhabitants of Fort Finis Terrae rushed to be first to use the lavatorium and got stuck in the doorway. "Line up in an orderly queue!" Bumptius commanded.

"Well done girl, that was a great job!" Brit said, popping a cabbage into Montana's mouth as a reward. "I wish you could stay here with us for ever."

Montana, in appreciation, trumpeted loudly from both ends.

CHAPTER SIX

Two months later, the snow had all gone. The daffodils were blooming and the days were growing longer and longer.

Brit and Drusilla stood on the fortress walls and stared out to sea. The Emperor's fleet was going to sail past today. One of the ships was coming to collect Montana.

"The Emperor still wants his favourite elephant to lead the triumphal birthday parade in Londinium," said Brit.

Festus leaped on the wall and barked. A whole forest of sails had appeared on the far horizon.

"Look!" said Drusilla. "I've never seen so many ships!"

"It's the Emperor's fleet!" Brit cheered.

"It looks like he's brought half of Rome with him!"

A two-masted cargo ship broke off from the fleet and sailed towards the quay, where Montana and the shipwrecked crew were waiting to be collected. Brit looked sadly on as the sailors hoisted his friend onto the ship, then climbed on board themselves.

They turned around and waved at the watching crowd, before putting up the sails and rejoining the waiting fleet.

Drusilla put her arm round Brit's shoulders. "Maybe they'll come back one day," she said. Brit nodded quietly.

She turned back to look at the fleet. "I wonder which one's the Emperor's ship."

Brit looked out too and pointed. "It must be that one," he said, squinting into the sunlight. "It's the biggest, and it's got gold all over it!"

A group of trumpeters stood on the prow of the ship. A fanfare drifted across the water. A tall man stood alone on the deck. The sun reflected brightly from his burnished, golden breastplate. He raised his hand in salute as the fleet drifted by.

"That's him!" Drusilla squeaked, waving with excitement. "It's the Emperor!"

The soldiers lined the battlements, saluting back to the Emperor. With one voice, they hailed their leader as he sailed past.

 The Emperor seemed to stare right at Brit. He smiled and touched a finger to his forehead in salute, as if he was thanking Brit for saving his favourite elephant.

Brit felt a surge of pride and pleasure flood through his body. *The Emperor is thanking me!* he thought.

Brit raised his hand and waved back as the Emperor and his fleet sailed away into the distance, on their way to Londinium.

A long, wailing trumpeting, that Brit
knew could only be the sound of an
elephant, floated through the air as the
ships became tiny dots on the horizon and
slowly disappeared from view.

He'd only known Montana for a couple of months, but he would miss her greatly. Now it was time to go home.

Together, Brit and Festus took the sheep back to the barn.

Brit put his arm round his faithful dog.

"At least I'll always have you, Festus," he smiled.

"Slurp!" said Festus, licking Brit's face with his long, wet, slobbery tongue.

ROMAN
BRIT

COLLECT THEM ALL!

Also available
as an ebook